Frindle

Nick, age 2 months

Frindle

ANDREW CLEMENTS

PICTURES BY BRIAN SELZNICK

ALADDIN PAPERBACKS

First Aladdin Paperbacks edition February 1998

Text copyright © 1996 by Andrew Clements
Illustrations copyright © 1996 by Brian Selznick

Aladdin Paperbacks
An imprint of Simon & Schuster Children's Publishing Division
1230 Avenue of the Americas
New York, NY 10020

Also available in a Simon & Schuster Books
for Young Readers hardcover edition.

The text of this book is set in 14-point Revival.
The illustrations are rendered in pencil.

Printed and bound in the United States of America

The Library of Congress has cataloged the hardcover edition as follows:
Clements, Andrew, 1949–
Frindle / by Andrew Clements; illustrations by Brian Selznick.
p. cm.
Summary: When he decides to turn his fifth grade teacher's love of the dictionary around on her, clever Nick Allen invents a new word and begins a chain of events that quickly moves beyond his control.
ISBN 0-689-80669-8
[1. Teacher-student relationships—Fiction. 2. Words, New—Fiction. 3. Schools—Fiction.] I. Selznick, Brian, ill. II. Title.
PZ7.C59118Fr 1996 95-26671
[Fic]—dc20

0-689-83861-1

For Becky, Charles, George, Nate, and John
—A. C.

one

Nick

IF YOU ASKED the kids and the teachers at Lincoln Elementary School to make three lists—all the really bad kids, all the really smart kids, and all the really good kids—Nick Allen would not be on any of them. Nick deserved a list all his own, and everyone knew it.

Was Nick a troublemaker? Hard to say. One thing's for sure: Nick Allen had plenty of ideas, and he knew what to do with them.

One time in third grade Nick decided to turn Miss Deaver's room into a tropical island. What kid in New Hampshire isn't ready for a little summer in February? So first he got everyone to make small palm trees out of green and brown construction paper and tape them onto the corners of each desk. Miss Deaver had only been a teacher for about six months, and she was delighted. "That's so *cute*!"

The next day all the girls wore paper flowers in their hair and all the boys wore sunglasses and beach hats. Miss Deaver clapped her hands and said, "It's so *colorful*!"

The day after that Nick turned the classroom thermostat up to about ninety degrees with a little screwdriver he had brought from home. All the kids changed into shorts and T-shirts with no shoes. And when Miss Deaver left the room for a minute, Nick spread about ten cups of fine white sand all over the classroom floor. Miss Deaver was surprised again at just how *creative* her students could be.

But the sand got tracked out into the hallway, where Manny the custodian did not think it was creative at all. And he stomped right down to the office.

The principal followed the trail of sand, and when she arrived, Miss Deaver was teaching the hula to some kids near the front of the room, and a tall, thin, shirtless boy with chestnut hair was just spiking a Nerf volleyball over a net made from six T-shirts tied together.

The third-grade trip to the South Seas ended. Suddenly.

But that didn't stop Nick from trying to liven things up. Lincoln Elementary needed a good jolt once in a while, and Nick was just the guy to deliver it.

About a year later, Nick made the great blackbird discovery. One night he learned on a TV show that red-wing blackbirds give this high-pitched chirp when a hawk or some other danger comes near. Because of the way sound travels, the hunter birds can't tell where the high-pitched chirp is coming from.

The next day during silent reading, Nick glanced at his teacher, and he noticed that Mrs. Avery's nose was curved—kind of like the beak of a hawk. So Nick let out a high, squeaky, blackbird "peep!"

Mrs. Avery jerked her head up from her book and looked around. She couldn't tell who did it, so she just said, "Shhh!" to the whole class.

A minute later Nick did it again, louder. "Peeep!" This time there was a little giggling from the class. But Mrs. Avery pretended not to hear the sound, and about fifteen seconds later she slowly stood up and walked to the back of the classroom.

Without taking his eyes off his book, and without moving at all, Nick put his heart and soul into the highest and most annoying chirp of all: "Peeeeep!"

Mrs. Avery pounced. "Janet Fisk, you stop that this instant!"

Janet, who was sitting four rows away from Nick, promptly turned white, then bright crimson.

"But it wasn't me . . . honest." There was a catch in Janet's voice, as if she might cry.

Mrs. Avery knew she had made a mistake, and she apologized to Janet.

"But someone is asking for big trouble," said Mrs. Avery, looking more like a hawk every second.

Nick kept reading, and he didn't make a peep.

At lunchtime Nick talked to Janet. He felt bad that Mrs. Avery had pounced on her. Janet lived in Nick's neighborhood, and sometimes they played together. She was good at baseball, and she was better at soccer than most of the kids in the whole school, boys or girls. Nick said, "Hey Janet—I'm sorry you got yelled at during reading. It was my fault.

I was the one who made that sound."

"You did?" said Janet. "But how come Mrs. Avery thought it was me?"

So Nick told her about the blackbirds, and Janet thought it was pretty interesting. Then she tried making a peep or two, and Janet's chirps were even higher and squeakier than Nick's. She promised to keep everything a secret.

For the rest of Nick's fourth-grade year, at least once a week, Mrs. Avery heard a loud "peeeep" from somewhere in her classroom—sometimes it was a high-pitched chirp, and sometimes it was a *very* high-pitched chirp.

Mrs. Avery never figured out who was making that sound, and gradually she trained herself to ignore it. But she still looked like a hawk.

To Nick, the whole thing was just one long—and successful—science experiment.

And Janet Fisk enjoyed it, too.

Mrs. Granger

FIFTH GRADE WAS different. That was the year to get ready for middle school. Fifth grade meant passing classes. It meant no morning recess. It meant real letter grades on your report cards. But most of all, it meant Mrs. Granger.

There were about one hundred fifty kids in fifth grade. And there were seven fifth-grade teachers: two math, two science, two social studies, but only one language arts teacher. In language arts, Mrs. Granger had a monopoly—and a reputation.

Mrs. Granger lived alone in a tidy little house in the older part of town. She drove an old, pale blue car to school every morning, rain or shine, snow or sleet, hail or wind. She had a perfect attendance record that stretched back farther than anyone could remember.

Her hair was almost white, swept away from her face and up into something like a nest on the back of her head. Unlike some of the younger women teachers, she never wore pants to school. She had two skirt-and-jacket outfits, her gray uniform and her blue uniform, which she always wore over a white shirt with a little cameo pin at the neck. And Mrs. Granger was one of those people who never sweats. It had to be over ninety degrees before she even took off her jacket.

She was small, as teachers go. There were even some fifth graders who were taller. But Mrs. Granger seemed like a giant. It was her eyes that did it. They were dark gray, and if she turned them on full power, they could make you feel like a speck of dust. Her eyes could twinkle and laugh, too, and kids said she could crack really funny jokes. But it wasn't the jokes that made her famous.

Everyone was sure that Mrs. Granger had X-ray vision. Don't even think about chewing a piece of gum within fifty feet of her. If you did, Mrs. Granger would see you and catch you and make you stick the gum onto a bright yellow index card. Then she would safety-pin the card to the front of your shirt, and you'd have to wear it for the rest of the school day. After that, you had to take it home and have your mom or dad sign the card, and bring it back to Mrs. Granger the next day. And it didn't matter to Mrs. Granger if you weren't in fifth grade, because the way she saw it, sooner or later, you would be.

All the kids at Lincoln Elementary School knew that at the end of the line—fifth grade—Mrs. Granger would be the one grading their spelling tests and their reading tests, and worst of all, their vocabulary tests—week after week, month after month.

Every language arts teacher in the world enjoys making kids use the dictionary: "Check your spelling. Check that definition. Check those syllable breaks."

But Mrs. Granger didn't just enjoy the dictionary. She *loved* the dictionary—almost worshipped it. Her weekly vocabulary list was thirty-five words long, sometimes longer.

As if that wasn't bad enough, there was a "Word for the Day" on the blackboard every morning. If you gave yourself a day off and didn't write one down and look it up and learn

Mrs. Granger loved the dictionary

the definition—sooner or later Mrs. Granger would find out, and then, just for you, there would be *two* Words for the Day for a whole week.

Mrs. Granger kept a full set of thirty dictionaries on a shelf at the back of the room. But her pride and joy was one of those huge dictionaries with every word in the universe in it, the kind of book it takes two kids to carry. It sat on its own little table at the front of her classroom, sort of like the altar at the front of a church.

Every graduate of Lincoln Elementary School for the past thirty-five years could remember standing at that table listening to Mrs. Granger's battle cry: "Look it up! That's why we have the dictionary."

Even before the school year started, when it was still the summer before fifth grade for Nick and his friends, Mrs. Granger was already busy. Every parent of every new fifth grader got a letter from her.

Nick's mom read part of it out loud during dinner one night in August.

Every home is expected to have a good dictionary in it so that each student

*can do his or her homework properly.
Good spelling and good grammar and
good word skills are essential for
every student. Clear thinking
requires a command of the English
language, and fifth grade is the ideal
time for every girl and boy to acquire
an expanded vocabulary.*

And then there was a list of the dictionaries
that Mrs. Granger thought would be "acceptable
for home study."

Mrs. Allen said, "It's so nice to have a
teacher who takes her work this seriously."

Nick groaned and tried to enjoy the rest of
his hamburger. But even watermelon for
dessert didn't cheer him up much.

Nick had no particular use for the dictionary. He liked words a lot, and he was good at
using them. But he figured that he got all the
words he needed just by reading, and he read
all the time.

When Nick ran into a word he didn't know,
he asked his brother or his dad or whoever was
handy what it meant, and if they knew, they'd
tell him. But not Mrs. Granger. He had heard
all about her, and he had seen fifth graders

in the library last year, noses stuck in their dictionaries, frantically trying to finish their vocabulary sheets before English class.

It was still a week before school and Nick already felt like fifth grade was going to be a very long year.

three

The Question

THE FIRST DAY of school was always a get-acquainted day. Books were passed out, and there was a lot of chatter. Everyone asked, "What did *you* do over the summer?"

Periods one through six went by very smoothly for Nick.

But then came period seven. Mrs. Granger's class was all business.

The first thing they did was take a vocabulary pretest to see how many of the thirty-five words for the week the kids already knew. *Tremble, circular, orchestra*—the list went on and on. Nick knew most of them.

Then there was a handout about class procedures. After that there was a review paper about cursive writing, and then there was a sample sheet showing how the heading should look on every assignment. No letup for thirty-seven minutes straight.

Nick was an expert at asking the delaying question—also known as the teacher-stopper, or the guaranteed-time-waster. At three minutes before the bell, in that split second between the end of today's class work and the announcement of tomorrow's homework, Nick could launch a question guaranteed to sidetrack the teacher long enough to delay or even wipe out the homework assignment.

Timing was important, but asking the right question—that was the hard part. Questions about stuff in the news, questions about the college the teacher went to, questions about the teacher's favorite book or sport or hobby—Nick knew all the tricks, and he had been very successful in the past.

Here he was in fifth grade, near the end of his very first language arts class with Mrs. Granger, and Nick could feel a homework assignment coming the way a farmer can feel a rainstorm.

Mrs. Granger paused to catch her breath, and Nick's hand shot up. She glanced down at her seating chart, and then up at him. Her sharp gray eyes were not even turned up to half power.

"Yes, Nicholas?"

"Mrs. Granger, you have so many dictionaries in this room, and that huge one especially . . . where did all those words come from? Did they just get copied from other dictionaries? It sure is a big book."

It was a perfect thought-grenade—KaPow!

Several kids smiled, and a few peeked at the clock. Nick was famous for this, and the whole class knew what he was doing.

Unfortunately, so did Mrs. Granger. She hesitated a moment, and gave Nick a smile that was just a little too sweet to be real. Her eyes were the color of a thundercloud.

"Why, what an interesting question, Nicholas. I could talk about that for hours, I bet." She glanced around the classroom. "Do the rest of you want to know, too?" Everyone nodded yes. "Very well then. Nicholas, will you do some research on that subject and give a little oral report to the class? If you find out the answer yourself, it will mean so much more than if I just told you. Please have your report ready for our next class."

Mrs. Granger smiled at him again. Very sweetly. Then it was back to business. "Now, the homework for tomorrow can be found on page twelve of your *Words Alive* book. . . ."

Nick barely heard the assignment. His heart was pounding, and he felt small, very small. He could feel the tops of his ears glowing red. A complete shutdown. An extra assignment. And probably a little black mark next to his name on the seating chart.

Everything he had heard about this teacher was true—don't mess around with The Lone Granger.

four

word Detective

IT WAS A BEAUTIFUL September afternoon, bright sun, cool breeze, blue sky. But not for Nick.

Nick had to do a little report for the next day. Plus copy out all the definitions for thirty-five words. For Mrs. Granger. This was not the way school was supposed to work. Not for Nick.

There was a rule at Nick's house: Homework First. And that meant right after school. Nick had heard his older brother, James, groan and grumble about this rule for years, right up until he graduated from high school two years ago. And then James wrote home from college after his first semester and said, "My grades are looking great, because when I came here I already knew how to put first things first." That letter was the proof Nick's mom and dad had been

Homework First

looking for. "Homework First" was the law from September to June.

This had never bothered Nick before because he hardly ever had homework. Oh sure, he looked over his spelling words on Thursday nights, and there had been a few short book reports in fourth grade, but other than that, nothing. Up to now, schoolwork never spilled over into his free time. Thanks to Mrs. Granger, those days were gone.

First he looked up the definitions in the brand-new red dictionary that his mom had bought—because Mrs. Granger told her to. It took almost an hour. He could hear a baseball game in John's yard down the street—yelling and shouting, and every few minutes the sharp crack of a bat connecting with a pitch. But he had a report to do. For Mrs. Granger.

Nick looked at the very front of the dictionary. There was an introduction to the book called "Words and Their Origins."

Perfect! Nick thought. It was just what he needed to do his report. It would all be over in a few minutes. Nick could already feel the sun and the breeze on his face as he ran outside to play, homework all done.

Then he read the first sentence from the introduction:

> *Without question this modern American dictionary is one of the most surprisingly complex and profound documents ever to be created, for it embodies unparalleled etymological detail, reflecting not only superb lexicographic scholarship, but also the dreams and speech and imaginative talents of millions of people over thousands of years—for every person who has ever spoken or written in English has had a hand in its making.*

What? Nick scratched his head and read it again. And then again. Not much better. It was sort of like trying to read the ingredients on a shampoo bottle.

He slammed the dictionary shut and walked downstairs.

Nick's family did a lot of reading, so bookshelves covered three of the four walls in the family room. There were two sets of encyclopedias—the black set was for grown-ups, and the red set was for kids. Nick pulled out the

D volume from the red set and looked up *dictionary*. There were three full pages, with headings like Early Dictionaries, Word Detectives, and Dictionaries Today. Not very exciting. But he had to do it, so Nick just plopped down on the couch and read all of it.

And when he was finished with the kids' book, he opened up the black encyclopedia and read most of what it said about dictionaries, too. He understood only about half of what he read.

He leaned back on the couch and covered his eyes with his arm, trying to imagine himself giving a report on all this boring stuff. He'd be lucky to have three minutes worth. But because Nick was Nick, he suddenly had an idea and it brought a grin to his face.

Nick decided that giving this report could actually be fun. He could make it into something special. After all, Mrs. Granger had asked for it.

five

The Report

BY LUNCHTIME the next day, Nick had a bad feeling in the pit of his stomach. Seventh period was coming. He was going to have to stand up in front of Mrs. Granger's class. The eyes of everyone in the class would be glued to his face. And Mrs. Granger's eyes would be cranked up to maximum punch power.

He looked over his notes again and again—the first English dictionary, the growth of the English language, William Shakespeare, words from French and German, new words, old words, new inventions, Anglo-Saxon words, Latin and Greek roots, American English—it all became a big jumble in his mind. And his grand plan from the night before? In the harsh fluorescent light of the school day, it seemed impossible.

What is it with the clocks in school? When you're planning to go to the carnival after school, the clocks in every class practically run backward, and the school day lasts for about three weeks. But if you have to go to the barber or go shopping for clothes after school, zzzzip— the whole day is over before you can blink. And today? After lunch, periods five and six went by in two ticks.

As the seventh-period bell rang, Mrs. Granger walked into the classroom, took four steps to her desk at the side of the room, flipped open her attendance book, glanced out at the class, and made two little check marks. Then looking up at Nick, she said, "I think we have a little report to begin our class today. Nicholas?"

Fifteen seconds into seventh period, and Nick was onstage. *This lady plays for keeps*, thought Nick. He gulped, grabbed his crumpled note cards and his book bag, and walked to the front of the room. He stood next to the giant dictionary on its little table, and Mrs. Granger walked to the back of the classroom and sat primly on a tall stool next to the bookcases. She was wearing her blue uniform.

Taking a deep breath, Nick began. "Well, the

first thing I learned is that the first English dictionary—"

Mrs. Granger interrupted. "Excuse me, Nicholas, but does your report have a title?"

Nick looked blankly at her. "A title? N-no, I didn't make a title."

"Class, please remember to include a title whenever you prepare an oral or written report. Now, please go on, Nicholas," and she smiled and nodded at him.

Nick began again. Looking right at Mrs. Granger he said, "The Dictionary." A couple of kids thought that was funny, but Nick played it straight, and just kept talking. "A lot of people think that the first English dictionary was put together in the 1700s by a man named Samuel Johnson. He lived in London, England. He was real smart, and he wrote a lot of books, and he wanted all the other smart people to have a good dictionary to use, so he made one. But there were other dictionaries before his. The thing that was different about Johnson's dictionary was its size, first of all. He had over forty-three thousand words in it."

The class made a bunch of noise at this big number—"Ooh," and "Wow!" and stuff like that—and Nick lost his concentration. He glanced up at Mrs. Granger, expecting to see those eyes drilling a hole in him. But they weren't. They were almost friendly, in a teacher-y kind of way. She shushed the class and said, "Go on, Nicholas. That's a fine beginning."

Nick almost smiled, but he saw all the kids staring at him, so he gripped his note cards even tighter, and jumped back in.

"The other thing that Samuel Johnson did that was special was to choose the words he thought were most important, and then give lots of examples showing how the words got used by people. For example, he showed how the word *take* could be used in one hundred thirteen different ways. . . ."

Nick's report went on smoothly for twelve minutes. Nick was surprised at how easy it was to stand there and talk about this stuff. At the end of the first five minutes Mrs. Granger had had to stop Nick again to say, "Class, it is not good manners to yawn out loud or to put your heads down on your desks when someone is giving an oral report." No one in the class cared one little bit about the report. Except Mrs. Granger.

Every time Nick glanced up, she was smiling.

And her eyes were not the least bit icy or sharp. She was eating this stuff up, listening, and nodding, and every once in a while she would say, "Very good point" or "Yes, that's exactly right."

But the next time Nick looked up, he saw Mrs. Granger sneaking a look at her watch. Eighteen minutes gone. Maybe his idea was going to work after all. Time for phase two.

Reaching into his book bag, Nick pulled out the red dictionary he had brought from home, the one most of the kids had—the one Mrs. Granger said they should use. Nick said, "This is the dictionary that I use at home for my vocabulary work, and . . . and I opened it up last night to the very front, and right there I found out a lot about how the dictionary was made . . . right in this book. So I thought some of the ideas would be good as part of my report. It says here . . ."

"Nicholas?" Nick looked up. Mrs. Granger got off her tall stool, and its wooden legs made a screech on the linoleum. Heads snapped to attention, and the class was alert again. Mrs. Granger smiled, raised her eyebrows and pointed at her watch. "Nicholas, I think the class should read that at home themselves. Now . . ."

John's hand was up in the air, and at Mrs. Granger's nod he said, "But I don't have that dictionary at home, Mrs. Granger. I have the blue one." And several other kids immediately said, "Me, too."

Mrs. Granger tried not to show that she was annoyed. "Very well, Nick, but it shouldn't take too long. We have other things to do today."

Nick kept his eyes open wide and nodded, adjusted his glasses on his nose, and began to read.

> *Without question this modern American dictionary is one of the most surprisingly complex and profound documents ever to be created, for it embodies unparalleled etymological detail, reflecting not only superb lexicographic scholarship, but also the dreams and speech and imaginative talents of millions of people over thousands of years—for every person who has ever spoken or written in English has had a hand in its making. . . .*

It was a long article, and the kids were bored to death. But no one looked bored at all. Every kid in the room knew now that the period was more than half over, and that Nick's report wasn't just a report. It was one of the greatest time-wasters he had ever invented.

Mrs. Granger knew it, too. She had edged around from the back of the room to the side near the windows. Nick glanced up at her now and then as he read, and each time, Mrs. Granger's eyes clicked up to a new power level. After eight minutes of Nick's best nonstop reading, her eyes were practically burning holes in the chalkboard behind him. There were only ten minutes left in seventh period.

When he took a breath to start a new paragraph, Mrs. Granger cut him off. "That's a fine place to stop, Nicholas. Class, let's all give him a round of applause for his report." The applause didn't last long.

As Nick took his book bag and notes and sat down, Mrs. Granger's eyes went back to almost normal, and she actually smiled at him. "Although your report was a little long—"she paused to let that sink in—"it was quite a good one. And isn't it fascinating that English has more different words than any other language used anywhere in the world?" She pointed at her large dictionary. "That one book contains the definitions of more than four-hundred fifty thousand words. Now, wasn't I right, Nicholas? All this will mean so much more since you learned about it on your own."

Mrs. Granger was beaming at him. Nick sank lower in his chair. This was worse than writing the report, worse than standing up to give it. He was being treated like—like the teacher's pet. And he had the feeling she was doing it on purpose. His reputation was in great danger. So he launched another question.

He raised his hand, and he didn't even wait for Mrs. Granger to call on him. "Yeah, but, you know, I still don't really get the idea of why words all mean different things. Like, who says that d-o-g means the thing that goes 'woof' and wags its tail? Who says so?"

And Mrs. Granger took the bait. "Who says *dog* means dog? You do, Nicholas. You and I and everyone in this class and this school and this town and this state and this country. We all agree. If we lived in France, we would all agree that the right word for that hairy four-legged creature was a different word—*chien*—it sounds like 'shee-en,' but it means what d-o-g means to

A. canis

B. chien

C. hund

1. 狗

2. cane

3. собáка

4. köpek

5. כלב

6. 犬

7. perro

8. σκύλος

9, 10. dog

11. كلب

Who says dog means dog?

you and me. And in Germany they say *hund*, and so on, all around the globe. But if all of us in this room decided to call that creature something else, and if everyone else did, too, then that's what it would be called, and one day it would be written in the dictionary that way. *We* decide what goes in that book." And she pointed at the giant dictionary. And she looked right at Nick. And she smiled again.

Then Mrs. Granger went on, "But of course, that dictionary was worked on by hundreds of very smart people for many years, so as far as we are concerned, that dictionary is the law. Laws can change, of course, but only if they need to. There may be new words that need to be made, but the ones in that book have been put there for good reasons."

Mrs. Granger took a look at the clock, eight minutes left. "Now then, for today you were to have done the exercises beginning on page twelve in your *Words Alive* book. Please get out your papers. Sarah, will you read the first sentence, identify the mistake, and then tell us how you corrected it?"

Mrs. Granger jammed the whole day's work into the last eight minutes, a blur of verbs and nouns and prepositions, and yes, there was another homework assignment.

And Nick didn't try to sidetrack Mrs. G. again. He had slowed her down a little, but had he stopped her? No way.

She was unstoppable . . . at least for today.

six

The Big Idea

THREE THINGS HAPPENED later that same afternoon.

Nick and Janet Fisk had missed the bus because of a school newspaper meeting, so they walked home together. They were seeing who could walk along the curb without falling. It took a lot of concentration, and when Janet stepped off into the street, Nick said, "That's three points for me."

But Janet said, "I didn't fall. I saw something. . . . Look." She bent down and picked up a gold ballpoint pen, the fancy kind.

That was the first thing—Janet finding the pen.

They got back on the curb, and Nick followed Janet, putting one foot carefully in front of the other on the narrow concrete curb.

And while he stepped along, he thought back over the school day, especially about his report. And what Mrs. Granger had said about words at the end of the period finally sank in.

That was the second thing—understanding what Mrs. Granger had said.

She had said, "Who says *dog* means dog? You do, Nicholas."

"You do, Nicholas," he repeated to himself.

I do? Nick thought, still putting one foot in front of the other, following Janet. *What does that mean?* And then Nick remembered something.

When he was about two years old, his mom had bought him one of those unbreakable cassette players and a bunch of sing-along tapes. He had loved them, and he played them over and over and over and over. He would carry the tape and the player to his mother or his big brother or his father and bang them together and say, "Gwagala, gwagala, gwagala," until someone put the cassette in the machine and turned it on.

And for three years, whenever he said "gwagala," his family knew that he wanted to hear those pretty sounds made with voices and instruments. Then when Nick went to preschool, he learned that if he wanted his teacher and the other kids to understand him, he had to use the word *music*. But *gwagala* meant that nice sound to Nick, because Nick said so. Who says *gwagala* means music? "You do, Nicholas."

"No fair!" yelled Janet. They were at the corner of their own street, and Nick had bumped into her, completely absorbed in his thoughts. Janet stumbled off the curb, and the gold pen in her hand clattered onto the street.

"Sorry . . . I didn't mean to, honest," said Nick. "I just wasn't watching. . . . Here . . ." Nick stooped over and picked up the pen and held it out to her. "Here's your . . ."

And that's when the third thing happened.

Nick didn't say "pen." Instead, he said, "Here's your . . . frindle."

"Frindle?" Janet took her pen and looked at him like he was nuts. She wrinkled her nose and said, "What's a *frindle?*"

Nick grinned and said, "You'll find out. See ya later."

It was there at the corner of Spring Street and South Grand Avenue, one block from home on a September afternoon. That's when Nick got the big idea.

The big idea

And by the time he had run down the street and up the steps and through the door and upstairs to his room, it wasn't just a big idea. It was a plan, a whole plan, just begging for Nick to put it into action. And "action" was Nick's middle name.

The next day after school the plan began. Nick walked into the Penny Pantry store and asked the lady behind the counter for a frindle.

She squinted at him. "A what?"

"A frindle, please. A black one," and Nick smiled at her.

She leaned over closer and aimed one ear at him. "You want *what?*"

"A frindle," and this time Nick pointed at the ballpoint pens behind her on the shelf. "A black one, please."

The lady handed Nick the pen. He handed her the 49¢, said "thank you," and left the store.

Six days later Janet stood at the counter of the Penny Pantry. Same store, same lady. John had come in the day before, and Pete the day before that, and Chris the day before that, and Dave the day before that. Janet was the fifth kid that Nick had sent there to ask that woman for a frindle.

And when she asked, the lady reached right for the pens and said, "Blue or black?"

Nick was standing one aisle away at the candy racks, and he was grinning.

Frindle was a real word. It meant *pen*. Who says frindle means pen? "You do, Nicholas."

Half an hour later, a group of serious fifth graders had a meeting in Nick's play room. It was John, Pete, Dave, Chris, and Janet. Add Nick, and that's six kids—six secret agents.

They held up their right hands and read the oath Nick had written out:

> *From this day on and forever, I will never use the word PEN again. Instead, I will use the word FRINDLE, and I will do everything possible so others will, too.*

And all six of them signed the oath—with Nick's frindle.

The plan would work.

Thanks, Mrs. Granger.

seven

word wars

SCHOOL WAS THE PERFECT place to launch a new word, and since this was a major historical event, Nick wanted it to begin in exactly the right class—seventh-period language arts.

Nick raised his hand first thing after the bell rang and said, "Mrs. Granger, I forgot my frindle."

Sitting three rows away, John blurted out, "I have an extra one you can borrow, Nick."

Then John made a big show of looking for something in his backpack. "I think I have an extra frindle, I mean, I told my mom to get me three or four. I'm sure I had an extra frindle in here yesterday, but I must have taken it . . . wait . . . oh yeah, here it is."

And then John made a big show of throwing it over to Nick, and Nick missed it on purpose.

Then he made a big show of finding it.

Mrs. Granger and every kid in the class got the message loud and clear. That black plastic thing that Nick borrowed from John had a funny name . . . a different name . . . a new name—*frindle*.

There was a lot of giggling, but Mrs. Granger turned up the power in her eyes and swept the room into silence. And the rest of the class went by according to plan—her plan.

As everyone was leaving after class, Mrs. Granger said, "Nicholas? I'd like to have . . . a word with you," and she emphasized the word *word*.

Nick's mouth felt dry, and he gulped, but his mind stayed clear. He walked up to her desk. "Yes, Mrs. Granger?"

"It's a funny idea, Nicholas, but I will not have my class disrupted again. Is that clear?" Her eyes were lit up, but it was mostly light, not much heat.

"Idea? What idea?" asked Nick, and he tried to make his eyes as blank as possible.

"You know what I mean, Nicholas. I am talking about the performance that you and John gave at the start of class. I am talking

40

about—this," and she held up her pen, an old maroon fountain pen with a blue cap.

"But I really didn't have a frindle with me," said Nick, amazed at his own bravery. And hiding behind his glasses, Nick kept his eyes wide and blank.

Mrs. Granger's eyes flashed, and then narrowed, and her lips formed a thin, hard line. She was quiet for a few seconds, and then she said, "I see. Very well. Then I guess we have nothing more to discuss today, Nicholas. You may go."

"Thanks, Mrs. Granger," said Nick, and he grabbed his backpack and headed for the door. And when he was just stepping into the hallway, he said, "And I promise I won't ever forget my frindle again. Bye."

eight

Mightier than the Sword

TWO DAYS LATER the photographer came to take class pictures. The fifth-grade picture would be taken last, right after lunch.

That gave Nick and his secret agents plenty of time, and they whispered something into the ear of every fifth grader. All the individual pictures had been taken, and finally it was time for the group picture. Everyone was lined up on the auditorium stage, everyone's hair looked great, and everyone was smiling.

But when the photographer said, "Say cheeese!"—no one did.

Instead, every kid said, "Frindle!" And they held one up for the camera to see.

The photographer was out of film. So that

shot was the only fifth-grade group picture he took. Six of the fifth-grade teachers were not pleased. And Mrs. Granger was furious.

No one had really wanted to make the teachers mad. It was just fun. It also got all the kids in the school talking about the new word. And when people pick up a new word, they say it all the time. The kids at Lincoln Elementary School liked Nick's new word. A lot.

But not Mrs. Granger. The day after the class picture she made an announcement to each of her classes, and she posted a notice on the main bulletin board by the office.

> *Anyone who is heard using the word* frindle *instead of the word* pen *will stay after school and write this sentence one hundred times: I am writing this punishment with a pen.*
>
> —*Mrs. Granger*

But that just made everyone want to use Nick's new word even more. Staying after school with The Lone Granger became a badge of honor. There were kids in her classroom every day after school. It went on like that for a couple of weeks.

One day near the end of seventh period, Mrs. Granger asked Nick to come talk to her after school. "This is not detention, Nicholas. I just want to talk."

Nick was excited. It was kind of like a conference during a war. One side waves a white flag, and the generals come out and talk. General Nicholas Allen. Nick liked the sound of it.

He stuck his head in Mrs. Granger's doorway after school. "You wanted to talk with me?"

"Yes, Nicholas. Please come in and sit down."

When he was settled she looked at him and said, "Don't you think this 'frindle' business has gone far enough? It's just a disruption to the school, don't you think?"

Nick swallowed hard, but he said, "I don't think there's anything wrong with it. It's just fun, and it really is a real word. It's not a bad word, just different. And besides, it's how words really change, isn't it? That's what you said."

Mrs. Granger sighed. "It *is* how a word could be made up brand new, I suppose, but the word *pen?* Should it really be replaced by . . . by that other word? The word *pen* has a long, rich history. It comes from the Latin word for feather, *pinna*. It started to become our word *pen* because quills made from feathers were some of the first writing tools ever made. It's a word that comes from somewhere. It makes *sense*, Nicholas."

"But *frindle* makes just as much sense to me," said Nick. "And after all, didn't somebody just make up the word *pinna*, too?"

That got a spark from Mrs. Granger's eyes, but all she said was, "Then you are not going to stop this?"

And Nick looked right in her eyes and said, "Well, me and . . . I mean, a bunch of my friends and I took an oath about using the word, and we have to keep our promise. And besides, I don't think there's anything wrong with it. I like my word." Nick tried to look brave, like a good general should.

"Very well then. I thought it would end up this way." Mrs. Granger pulled a fat white envelope from her desk drawer and held it up. "This is a letter I have written to you, Nicholas."

Nick held out his hand, thinking she was going to give it to him. But she didn't.

"I am not going to send it to you until all this is over. I want you to sign your name and put

Like a conference during a war

today's date across the back of the envelope. When you read it, whenever that may be, you will know it is the same letter, and that I have not made any changes to it."

"This is weird," Nick said to himself. But to Mrs. Granger he said, "Sure," and he signed his name in his best cursive, and put the date under it.

Then Mrs. Granger stood up abruptly and said, "Then that is all for today, Nicholas. And may the best word win."

There was a frown on her face, but her eyes, her eyes were different—almost happy.

And Nick was halfway down the hall before it hit him—"She likes this war, and she wants to win real bad!"

Walking to school the next day, Pete had a great idea. "How 'bout we see if we can get every kid in the whole fifth grade to go up and ask Mrs. Granger, 'Can I borrow a frindle?'"

"You mean 'Mrs. Granger, *may* I borrow a frindle?'" said Dave. "Got to use good grammar. Don't wanna upset Dangerous Grangerous."

"Sounds good to me," said Nick. "She can't keep everyone after school, can she?"

Almost eighty kids stayed after school with Mrs. Granger that day. They filled her room and spilled out into the hallway. The principal had to stay late to help, and they had to arrange two special late buses to get all the kids home.

And the next day, all the fifth graders did it again, and so did a lot of other students—over two hundred kids.

Parents called to complain. The school bus drivers threatened to go on strike. And then the school board and the superintendent got involved.

And about this time the principal of Lincoln Elementary School paid a little visit to the home of Mr. and Mrs. Allen. She wanted to talk to them about their son. The one in fifth grade. The one named Nick.

nine

Chess

MRS. MARGARET CHATHAM had been principal of Lincoln Elementary School for eighteen years. She knew Mr. and Mrs. Allen, because they had all served together on the building committee when the old Lincoln School was torn down and the new one was built six years ago.

When she telephoned on the afternoon of October first to set up the meeting, Mrs. Chatham had asked Nick to be there, too. It was 6:30 when she knocked, and Nick opened the door.

"Good evening, Nick," she said. No smile.

"Hi, Mrs. Chatham," said Nick, backing away as she filled the doorway. She was a large person, as tall as Nick's dad, with wide shoulders. Nick guessed she would play linebacker on

The game was not over

a football team, because that's what his dad had played in college.

"Hello, Mr. and Mrs. Allen," she said, stepping into the living room. She was wearing a long black raincoat with a red silk scarf tied loosely around her neck. She kept her coat on, but took off the scarf and tucked it into her left pocket. She shook hands stiffly with both of Nick's parents before sitting down on the chair to the left of the couch. Nick's mom and dad sat on the couch, and Nick sat on the rocking chair that faced Mrs. Chatham across the low coffee table.

"This is not an easy visit for me. We are having some trouble at school, and it appears that Nick is in the middle of it."

Then while Nick's parents listened, Mrs. Chatham laid out the story as she saw it—Nick encouraging the other kids to use his new word, Mrs. Granger forbidding it, the ruined fifth-grade class picture, hundreds of kids staying after school, and a general feeling that there was a rebellion at school, with no one respecting the rules anymore.

Nick watched his mom and dad while Mrs. Chatham talked, looking from one face to another. His dad was listening carefully, nodding and frowning. He looked embarrassed about the trouble. But his mom looked—kind of annoyed.

And when Mrs. Chatham finished her story, Nick's mom was the first one to speak. "But doesn't all this seem like a lot of fuss about something pretty silly?"

Nick sat quietly, but in his mind he shouted, *Hurrah for mom, hurrah for mothers everywhere!* His mom wasn't annoyed with him! She was annoyed with Mrs. Granger, maybe even annoyed with Mrs. Chatham. This was getting interesting.

Mrs. Allen was still talking to the principal. "I mean, is there really any harm in the children making up a funny word and saying it? Does there have to be a rule that a word like this may not be used?"

Mrs. Chatham sighed and said, "Yes, I suppose it does seem silly. But Mrs. Granger thinks that it's rather like keeping children from saying 'ain't'—there have to be standards. That's why we have dictionaries. And really, the problem isn't so much the word itself. It's the lack of respect for authority."

Mr. Allen said, "Mrs. Granger's right about

that. There have to be standards. We can't have kids walking around saying 'ain't,' can we?"

And that's when Nick piped in. "You know that big dictionary in Mrs. Granger's room? The word *ain't* is right there in the book. I looked it up, and there it was. I don't see why I can't use a word if it's in the dictionary. Mrs. Granger even said that her big dictionary was the law." Nick looked from face to face to face. That stumped them all. He had just launched a first-class thought-grenade.

"Well, yes . . . but . . . well, as I said, the word *ain't* and even the word *frindle*—these are not the real issue here," said Mrs. Chatham.

Mrs. Allen said, "Well, I think the real issue is Mrs. Granger's reaction to a harmless little experiment with language—it's an overreaction, don't you think so, Tom?" And Mrs. Allen looked at her husband.

It was Mr. Allen's turn to look from face to face to face. He was lost. "Yes, well sure . . . I—I guess so . . . I mean, it's not like anybody's been hurt . . . umm . . . I mean, it's not like vandalism or stealing or something like that . . ." His sentence trailed off, and he rubbed his chin and stared thoughtfully through the window on the wall behind Mrs. Chatham.

And while the three grown-ups sat there in an uncomfortable moment of silence, Nick had a sudden vision of what was really going on here. It was a chess game, Nick against Mrs. Granger. Mrs. Granger had just tried to end the game by using her queen—Mrs. Chatham in her black raincoat, the black queen.

Nick didn't know it until the attack was under way, but he had a powerful defender of his own—good old Mom, the white queen. And the game was not over. It would go on until there was a winner and a loser.

Mrs. Chatham didn't stay much longer. There was a little more talk back and forth across the chessboard about how children have a right to explore new ideas, about the importance of respecting teachers and the work they do, about everybody needing to keep up standards and make school a safe place to learn.

Then Mr. Allen offered Mrs. Chatham some coffee and banana bread, but she said, "No thanks, I really must be going now."

She thanked Nick's parents and they thanked her. Nick opened the door, and said, "Good night, Mrs. Chatham." Then the black queen put on her red scarf and walked off into the October twilight.

"Nick, I think we'd better talk a little more about this," said his mom, sitting back down on the couch. "If I find out that you have been disrespectful to Mrs. Granger or any other teacher at school, then you really will be in big trouble."

"I haven't been disrespectful. Honest. I did get everybody started using my word, but like you said, it's not hurting anybody. And I'm sorry if me and Dave and Pete got everybody to ask Mrs. Granger to borrow a frindle. That was mean, I guess . . . but she started it by making kids stay after school and write a hundred sentences just for saying my word once. All the kids like to use my word. It's just fun, that's all."

"Well," said Nick's dad, "if it gets everyone upset and makes the principal come talk to your mother and me, then it must not be fun for everybody, is it? And I think you should just tell all your friends to knock it off, right now . . . I mean, tomorrow."

Nick shook his head. "I can't, Dad. It won't work. It's a real word now. It used to be just mine, but not anymore. If I knew how to stop it, I think I probably would. But I can't." And Nick looked at both of their faces to see if that idea was sinking in. It was. "Like I said, I won't be disrespectful, but I do like my word. And I guess now we're just going to have to see what happens."

And the chessmen—Nick's king and queen—had to agree.

The game would go on.

ten

Freedom of the Press

JUDY MORGAN WAS a reporter for *The Westfield Gazette*, the local newspaper. Westfield was a quiet little town. There was the occasional burglary, the teenagers got rowdy once in a while, and there was some shouting at the town council or the planning board now and then. But mostly, things were calm and orderly in Westfield, and every Thursday *The Westfield Gazette* proved it.

Ted Bell sold advertisements for the paper, and he had a daughter in fourth grade at Lincoln Elementary. He told Judy that a bunch of fifth graders were making trouble and were not obeying teachers anymore, that there was something about a secret code word they were all using.

And half the students had been kept after school one day last week—including his own little girl.

The only other story Judy was working on was about eighteen new trees that were going to be planted along East Main Street. The trees could wait. This thing at the elementary school sounded like a real story.

So Judy Morgan showed up at Lincoln Elementary School at three o'clock the day after Mrs. Chatham had been to visit Nick's parents. The sign on the door said, "All Visitors Must Report to the Office," and she did.

On the bulletin board outside the office, Judy saw Mrs. Granger's notice about the punishment for using the word *frindle*. She stepped back two paces, aimed her camera at the notice, and snapped a photo. She read the notice once more, and then stepped into the office.

Mrs. Freed, the school secretary, looked up and smiled. "May I help you?"

"Yes, I'm sure you can. My name is Judy Morgan, and I work for *The Westfield Gazette*. I'd like to know about that poster outside the office, the one about this word *frindle*. Who should I talk to?"

Mrs. Freed stopped smiling. She was sick and tired of anything to do with that word. For the past week her phone had been ringing off the hook. If it wasn't a parent complaining about a child who had to stay after school, it was someone from the school board trying to get in touch with Mrs. Chatham or Mrs. Granger. Mrs. Freed pursed her lips and narrowed her eyes. She said, "You'll have to speak with the principal. Let me see if Mrs. Chatham is free."

She was. There isn't a principal alive who won't find the time to talk to someone from the local newspaper. The reporter was invited into Mrs. Chatham's office.

Judy noticed right away that the principal was not comfortable talking about this stuff. When asked about the poster outside the office door, Mrs. Chatham laughed and said, "Oh, that? It's nothing really. Some kids have been playing a prank, and it was time to put a stop to it."

The principal's laugh sounded phony to Judy Morgan. "And did that notice put an end to the prank? I heard that a lot of children were kept after school last week. Would you tell me a little about that? Parents would like to know what's going on."

Mrs. Chatham looked like . . . well, like a kid who had been sent to the principal's office. She squirmed a little in her chair and tried to smile. She said, "Well, we do still have a little problem, but it's under control. Mrs. Granger may have overreacted a bit. I don't think the children have really been trying to be disrespectful. They are just having some fun, and it's more like a difference of opinion . . ." And then Mrs. Chatham went on to tell the reporter what she knew about the word *frindle*, and how it had become popular among the students. Judy Morgan took careful notes.

And when the principal had finished Judy said, "Would you mind if I asked Mrs. Granger a few questions?"

Mrs. Chatham said, "No, not at all." But Judy could tell that the principal wished she would just go away. What could she say, though? Mrs. Chatham couldn't very well keep the reporter away from Mrs. Granger because, after all, America is a free country with a free press. If Judy really wanted to, she would talk to Mrs. Granger sooner or later.

It was sooner. In three minutes Judy Morgan was standing at the doorway of Room

12, looking in at Mrs. Granger. There were about fifteen children sitting at desks scattered around the room, busy writing out their one hundred sentences. She knocked and the teacher and students looked up from their work. "I'm Judy Morgan from *The Westfield Gazette*, Mrs. Granger. May I have a word with you?"

Mrs. Granger stood and came out into the hallway and closed the door. Judy could see past her and saw that every kid in the room was straining to listen. Judy noticed Mrs. Granger's eyes right away—gray, maybe flecked with a little gold, and very sharp, but not hard or mean. Just bright, and strong.

The reporter didn't waste words. "So I hear that you plan to stop the students from using their new word. How goes the battle?"

Mrs. Granger did not smile, and her eyes got even brighter. "First of all, it is not a battle. I am merely helping my students to see that this foolishness should stop. Such a waste of time and thought! There is no reason to invent a new and useless word. They should each learn to use the words we already have. But of course, all of this is just a silly fad, and when you add an *e* to *fad*, you get *fade*.

And I predict that this fad will fade."

Judy looked up from her note pad and asked, "Any idea how it all got started?"

Mrs. Granger's eyes seemed to almost catch on fire at that question, and she said, "Yes, I have a *very* good idea how it all got started. It was one young man's idea, a fifth-grade student named Nicholas Allen. And now you will have to excuse me, Ms. Morgan, for I have papers I must grade." And with a brief, firm handshake, Mrs. Granger ended the interview.

The reporter didn't leave right away. She walked back through the hallway and sat on a bench outside the office so she could look over her notes to make sure they made sense. It took her about five minutes. Then Judy stood up, put her notebook into her large black purse, waved good-bye to a frowning Mrs. Freed, and headed out the door.

As she walked to the parking lot, five or six kids who had just finished writing their sentences for Mrs. Granger came out another door. Judy walked beside them, listening to them laugh and joke. Then she asked them, "Why do you kids keep saying 'frindle'? Don't you hate staying after school?"

A boy who was almost falling over from the weight of his backpack looked up at her and smiled. "It's not so bad. There's always a bunch of my friends there. I've written that sentence six hundred times now."

And then the kids said Mrs. Granger didn't even look at their punishment papers anymore. They were sure, because where you were supposed to write "I am writing this punishment with a pen," everyone was writing the word *frindle* every fourth or fifth sentence. And Mrs. Granger hadn't said anything. One girl bragged that she had written the word *frindle* forty-five times on her sheets today. She grinned and said, "That's a new record."

"And this boy named Nick," Judy asked, "has he had to stay after school, too?"

The kids giggled, and a tall boy with reddish-brown hair and glasses said, "Mrs. Granger has kept Nick after school so much that everyone thinks she wants to adopt him."

The reporter smiled and said, "Do you think I could find Nick and talk to him this afternoon?"

The boy looked at Judy for a second, and then said, "I don't think Nick would want to

That's a new record

talk to you right now. He might say something stupid and get himself in trouble." Then he grinned at his friends. The kids laughed and poked and punched each other, and headed off down the block. Judy drove back to her office and started writing.

The next morning a brown envelope arrived at the *Gazette* offices addressed to Judy Morgan, and below her name was written "Frindle Story." When Judy opened it, there was a class picture, the fifth grade at Lincoln Elementary School. Mrs. Granger and the six other teachers were standing at the ends of the rows and the kids were dressed neatly, hair all combed. But there was something odd about the picture.

The reporter looked closely and saw that each kid was holding up a pen, and each little mouth was puckered in the same way. She was puzzled for a second, but then she said softly, "Of course! They're all saying 'frindle'!"

Written on the back of the picture in neat cursive was "3rd row, 5th from left."

Judy looked at the picture, and there she saw the same grinning red-haired boy with glasses that she had talked to in the school parking lot yesterday. She chuckled and said, "Well, well, well. Pleased to meet you, Mr. Nicholas Allen."

eleven

Extra! Extra! Read All About It!

ON THURSDAY MORNING, *The Westfield Gazette* was delivered to all 12,297 homes and post office boxes in Westfield. The story about Lincoln Elementary School was the first item on the front page. And the headline?

Local 5th Grader Says, "Move over, Mr. Webster"

It was quite an article. Not that Judy Morgan didn't tell the truth—every statement in the article was completely true. It was the particular way she told the truth that got things hopping around town.

For example, take this sentence about Mrs. Granger: "Mrs. Granger, champion of the forces of order and authority, is battling hundreds of young frindle-fighters. Neither side is giving in."

Or this bit about Nick: "Everyone agrees that Nick Allen masterminded this plot that cleverly raises issues about free speech and academic rules. He is the boy who invented the new word."

Or this last sentence in the article: "One thing is sure: the kids at Lincoln Elementary School love their frindles, and no one seems to be backing off in this war of the words."

And of course *The Westfield Gazette* published the class picture, too. And Mrs. Granger and Nick were identified for all the world to see.

"What is the meaning of this?!" That's what Nick's mother said, putting the article in front of Nick's nose when he got home from school. "Did you talk to this reporter? She seems to know an awful lot about you and your new word, young man!"

"What is the meaning of this?!" That's what the school superintendent said to Mrs. Chatham, slapping a copy of the article onto her desk. "Why did you have to talk to that reporter? Don't we have enough trouble getting the taxpayers to pay for the schools without articles like this banging around town?!"

"What is the meaning of this?!" That's what Mrs. Chatham said to Mrs. Granger, shaking the newspaper in front of her face. "I know you had to talk to that woman, but did you have to say all these things? It'll be a wonder if we don't all get fired!"

It was quite a Thursday for everyone. And no one could figure out how Judy Morgan had gotten that fifth-grade class picture.

twelve

Airwaves

WITHIN A WEEK after the article was published in *The Westfield Gazette*, the kids at the junior high and the kids at the high school had stopped using the word *pen* and had started using the word *frindle*. They loved it.

Nick became sort of a hero for kids all over town, and he quickly learned that being a hero—even if you're only a local hero—isn't a free ride. It has a price.

People noticed Nick when he walked into his dad's hardware store or when he stood in line at the Penny Pantry to buy a candy bar. He could feel it when someone recognized him, and it made him shy and awkward.

Kids at school started expecting him to be clever and funny all the time, and even for a kid as smart as Nick, that was asking a lot. Every teacher, the office secretary, the principal, even the school nurse and the custodian, all seemed to be watching, always watching.

His parents were great about everything. True, his mom had been upset when the article first came out, and so had his dad. Nick had said, "But I didn't do anything wrong, Mom. And neither did that lady from the newspaper." And his parents could see that he was right. The things in the article were true, and the truth is the truth, and nothing could be done about it now. Even though it made them uncomfortable to have their boy talked about all over town, secretly, Nick's mom and dad were pleased. After all, a brand-new word is a pretty amazing thing. Their Nicholas was quite a fellow—no getting around it.

Someone else in town thought this brand-new word was pretty amazing, too. Bud Lawrence had lived all his life in Westfield, and when he was only nineteen years old, he had saved enough money to make an investment. He looked around for a good idea, and then bought the first Dairy Queen in the state. After a few years he bought a McDonald's restaurant. That was almost thirty years ago, and these two restaurants had made him rich, one of Westfield's leading citizens.

When Bud Lawrence saw the article about the new word, he had his lawyer file a preliminary trademark claim on the word *frindle*. Within four days he had set up a small company that was selling cheap plastic ballpoint pens specially imprinted with the word *frindle*. He sold three thousand *frindles* the first week, and they sold so fast that stores all over Westfield couldn't keep them in stock. Then just as quickly, kids stopped asking for frindles. The sales slowed down, and Bud Lawrence started thinking about other projects.

A week later it was Halloween, the leaves started falling, and it seemed like the town was going to quiet down.

And it would have—if it hadn't been for Alice Lunderson. Alice lived in Betherly, a town seven miles away from Westfield, and she worked part time for the local CBS-TV station in Carrington, a town of about 75,500 people.

When there was important area news—disasters like floods or tornadoes—or sometimes if she came across little stories that seemed cute or original, Alice would call the station news manager in Carrington. If it was a good story or if it was a day when not much else was happening in the world, then the TV station would send out a van with a camera crew to shoot some videotape.

Alice subscribed to all the small-town newspapers in the area to keep up with local events. Most of them were published on Thursday, and they arrived at her house by Monday or Tuesday. Then it took her a day or so to look through them all. On Wednesday morning she finally saw the article in *The Westfield Gazette* about the word war. She read it through twice, and looked carefully at the class photograph. She was sure that this story was a winner.

The TV station manager in Carrington agreed with her. He called the CBS station in Boston, because sometimes Boston picked up stories from the Carrington newsroom. The woman in Boston thought the story had some real zip to it, so she called the network news editor in New York.

When the fax of *The Westfield Gazette* article got to New York, the staff there loved it. They looked over the schedule sheet for the week and decided it would be the perfect closing story for the CBS evening news for the next day, Thursday. Orders flew back through the telephone links from New York to Boston to Carrington to Betherly. By Wednesday at noon, Alice had a "go" order to take the story all the way. It was her first piece to get onto the national news, and twenty million viewers would see it.

Alice Lunderson and her camera crew stood on Mrs. Granger's front porch Wednesday after school. Mrs. Granger was not impressed at all by the lights and the microphones. She looked right into the camera and said, "I have always said that the dictionary is the finest tool ever made for educating young minds, and I still say that. Children need to understand that there are rules about words and language, and that those rules have a history that makes sense. And to pretend that a perfectly good English word can be replaced by a silly made-up word just for the fun of it, well, it's not something I was ready to stand by and watch without a fight."

"And have you lost that fight, Mrs. Granger?" asked the reporter.

Mrs. Granger turned her eyes up to nearly full power as she looked into the camera, and with a pale smile she said, "It's not over yet."

When Alice and the crew showed up at Nick's house, the Allen family was ready for them. Mom and Dad sat on the couch with Nick between them. Nick squinted into the lights. His mom had worked out with Nick what he could say and what he couldn't say. "You remember, young man," she had told him as she combed his hair, "these reporters are just looking for a quick story that will make some excitement. But you have to stay here and live in this town. So mind your Ps and Qs."

As they sat there on the couch, Mrs. Allen had her foot on top of Nick's under the coffee table, and if she pushed down, it meant that the reporter had just asked a question that she was going to answer for him. Mrs. Allen did not trust reporters.

"So tell me, Nick, why did you make up this new word, *frindle?*" asked Alice Lunderson.

Nick gulped and said, "Well, my teacher Mrs. Granger said that all the words in the dictionary were made up by people, and that they mean what they mean because we say they do. So I thought it would be fun to just make up a new word and see if that was true."

"And were you surprised when Mrs. Granger got mad about that?" asked Alice with a smile.

There was a push on Nick's foot and his mother said, "We never felt that Mrs. Granger got angry. When everyone started using the word *frindle*, it just got to be a disruption, that's all. She's really a very fine teacher."

"Yeah," said Nick. "I mean, I learned a lot about words, and without her, I wouldn't have."

"So what's next for you and the new word?" Alice was wrapping it up. She could see that Nick and his parents were not going to be pushed into saying anything controversial. So she just kept it light and happy.

"Well," said Nick, "the funny thing is, even though I invented it, it's not my word anymore. *Frindle* belongs to everyone now, and I guess everyone will figure out what happens together."

Alice also had a short chat with a worried looking Mrs. Chatham, and a smiling Bud Lawrence, maker of the official *frindle*. Then she shot her opening bit and her closing bit, and the camera crew drove back to Carrington to edit all the pieces and put them together into a two-minute news story.

The next night, when all the serious news about wars and oil prices and world food supplies had been talked about on the CBS evening news, the anchorman looked into the camera and smiled.

He said, "It is believed by many that the word *quiz* was made up in 1791 by a Dublin theater manager named Daly. He had bet someone that he could invent a brand-new word in the English language, and he chalked up the letters *q-u-i-z* onto every wall and building in town. The next morning, there it was, and within a week people all over Ireland were wondering what it could mean—and a new word had been created. *Quiz* is the only word in English that was invented by one person for no particular reason—that is until now. Now there is a new word, *frindle*, and here is Alice Lunderson in Westfield, New Hampshire, with the story."

Alice came on the screen with a short introduction. Then, right there on TV, Mrs. Granger and Nick and Bud Lawrence and Nick's mom were talking to twenty million people about frindles.

One of those twenty million people was a producer for the *Late Show with David*

Letterman. And another one of those twenty million people was a staff writer for *People* magazine, and another one was a writer for *3-2-1 Contact* magazine for kids. Dozens of other writers and producers and marketing people saw that story on the news—and all of them smelled a great story.

During the next three weeks every man, woman, and child in America heard about this funny new word that kids were using instead of the word *pen*. And kids in Ohio and Iowa and New York and Texas and California started using it, too.

Bud Lawrence was suddenly flooded with orders for anything with the word *frindle* on it, and he quickly got interested again. But there were complications.

Bud's lawyer said, "You see that stack of orders there? Trouble. That's what that is. We got a trademark filed, but it's only like an application. The whole country knows that that little kid made up the word, and unless you make a deal with his dad, you're going to end up with nothing—maybe even a big fat lawsuit. That kid owns that word."

When Mr. Allen came home at lunchtime,

America heard about this funny new word

his wife told him that he had to call Bud Lawrence. "It's something about the new word."

This was not good news to Tom Allen. He was sick and tired of all the fuss. And being away from the hardware store so much while all this nonsense was happening had put him weeks behind on his paperwork. He'd be lucky now to get his Christmas order in time.

Even though he didn't really want anything to do with it, Bud was an old friend. So on the way back to the store, Nick's dad went to Bud Lawrence's office.

"Tom—good to see you," said Bud. He stood up and walked around his desk to shake hands. "Have a seat." Tom sat down uneasily, and Bud pulled another chair over. "Ever seen Westfield so stirred up about anything in your life? You and Ginny must be pretty proud of . . . that boy of yours." Bud couldn't remember Nick's name.

Tom shifted in his chair and nodded. "Yes, he's quite something, that's for sure. But I tell you, Bud, I'm ready for it all to just die down and blow away—too much fuss."

Instantly, Bud saw how to get what he wanted. "Well, Tom, I'm afraid it's not really going to go away. Looks like something's started up, and people are real interested. You probably saw those bright red ballpoints around town with the word *frindle* on 'em? That was my doing. Just testing the waters. But your boy, he owns that word. I got my lawyer to apply for a trademark a few weeks back, because that's just the way I am. New thing comes along, I like to be right there in the middle of it." He grinned at Tom Allen, and Tom smiled back weakly.

"Right now, I got a shirt printer in Massachusetts and another one in Chicago and another one in Los Angeles making T-shirts with the word *frindle* above a picture of a pen—I mean a frindle. Each supplier has orders so far for over twenty thousand shirts. Profit on every one of those is going to be two, maybe three dollars. And I'm talking with some big pen and pencil companies in Hong Kong and Japan about a deal that could be worth some really big money. They've seen this frindle thing in the media, and they want to buy the rights to the trademark and make a new line of frindles for kids. I'm not kidding—this is a hot, hot idea!"

Bud guessed right. Just the thought of all this made Tom shrink back uncomfortably in his chair. It was way too much fuss.

"Tom, let me be direct with you. As the boy's guardian, you need to do the right thing about all this. I'd like to see where all this is going to go. I'm going to take some risks, spend some money, see what happens. But I need your permission. I need your signature on these trademark papers, and I need to strike a deal with you about permission to use that trademark. I know it seems like a big ruckus about a word, but we just can't tell what's to come of it unless we take some steps." Bud pointed at the papers on his desk. "That's a contract, and it's fair and honest. It gives your boy thirty percent of whatever profits I might make. That's a fair royalty, generous for this kind of deal. So what do you say—make sense? Let me take care of all the fuss, and see if some good doesn't maybe come of it all?" The papers and a pen were there on the desk next to Tom.

He looked at Bud, then reached over, picked up the pen, and signed both copies of the trademark papers and three copies of the contract. "I've got no reason to doubt you one bit, Bud, and I sure don't want to mess with any of this myself. Is that it?" he asked, standing up.

"Not quite, Tom. Here." Then Bud Lawrence

handed Nick's dad a check for $2,250.

"What's this for?"

"That's what I owe Nick for the sales of frindles from the first three weeks," explained Bud with a smile.

Tom looked at the check and said, "This is terrific, Bud, and I'm really glad about it because it'll sure help with Nick's college. But I wish you'd just keep this between us. If Nick knew, he'd probably stop mowing lawns and I'd never get him to save another penny. So just between us, okay?"

Bud said, "Sure, Tom, I understand. Just between us." And they shook hands.

Mr. Allen left Bud's office and walked across the street to the savings bank. He set up a trust account for Nick, and the bank manager said he could make arrangements with Mr. Lawrence so any other money would be deposited automatically. That sounded good to Tom Allen. If he never heard another word about it, that would be fine.

As Nick's dad walked slowly back to the hardware store, he wondered if things were ever going to be the same again in his quiet little town.

thirteen

Ripples

BUT LIFE DID SETTLE back to normal in Westfield. More leaves fell, Thanksgiving came, then the first snow, then Christmas, and more snow. Fall and winter seemed to calm everything down and drive everyone into their own houses.

Things were calmer at Lincoln Elementary School, too. Frindle-mania was over. But that didn't mean the word was gone. Not at all.

All the kids and even some of the teachers used the new word. At first it was on purpose. Then it became a habit, and by the middle of February, *frindle* was just a word, like *door* or *tree* or *hat*. People in Westfield barely noticed it anymore.

But in the rest of the country, things were hopping. Frindle was on the move. In hundreds of little towns and big cities from coast to coast, kids were using the new word, and parents and teachers were trying to stop it. What had happened in Westfield happened over and over and over again.

Bud Lawrence couldn't have been happier. There were frindle shirts and sunglasses and erasers and notebooks and paper and dozens of other items. The new line of frindles imported from Japan were a big hit, and now there was talk of selling them in Japan and Europe, as well. The checks that went into Nick's trust fund got bigger and bigger.

Bud opened his own factory in Westfield to make frindle baseball caps, which created jobs for twenty-two people. And in March the town council voted to put up a little sign on the post below the town's name along Route 302. It said, "Home of the Original Frindle."

And Mrs. Granger? She seemed to have given up, or perhaps she had been ordered to. No one knew. Her poster about the forbidden word had quietly disappeared from the bulletin board, and kids were not staying after school writing sentences anymore. It was business as usual.

Except for one thing.

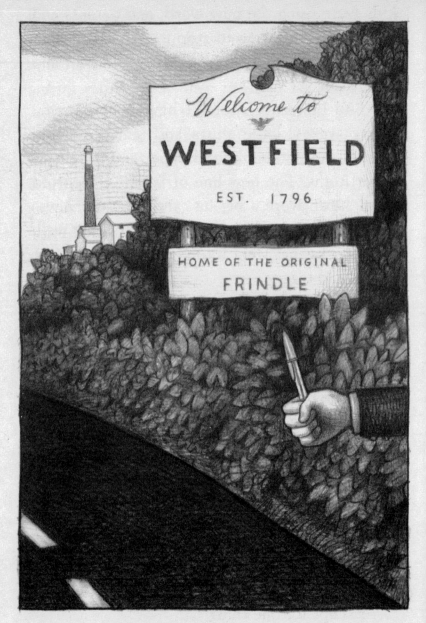

But life did settle back to normal

Everyone in fifth grade got at least one word wrong on his or her spelling test each week. Every week, the first word at the top of Mrs. Granger's list was *pen*. And each Friday during the spelling test, every kid spelled it *f-r-i-n-d-l-e*.

Nick was sort of a celebrity for a while. Everyone had seen him on *The Late Show*, and on *Good Morning, America* and two or three other TV shows. John and Chris and all his friends kept asking about what it was like to ride in a limousine. After a week or two, though, it was old news, and everyone seemed to forget it and move on.

The only person who couldn't quite forget about everything was Nick.

fourteen

Inside Nick

ON THE OUTSIDE, Nick was still Nick. But inside, it was different. Oh sure, he still had a lot of great ideas, but now they scared him a little.

For instance, Nick learned in social studies class that people who buy stuff are called *consumers*. If consumers stop buying, stores and shops and restaurants go out of business.

Then—boom—a new idea hit him.

All the kids loved lunchtime. But the awful part about lunch was the eating part—school food. And the food was never a surprise—you had to smell it all morning and then go eat it. The food was always bad.

Well, thought Nick, *the school cafeteria is sort of a restaurant, isn't it? And the students are the consumers, right? And we don't really have to buy our lunches there, do we?*

Nick could see it all: He would get all the kids to bring their lunches from home every day until the ladies who made the lunches cooked better food. He was sure those women didn't cook food like that for their own families. The kids were the consumers with $1.35 in their pockets, and until the food was better, that's where their money would stay.

Great idea! Nick was sure it would work, and he got all excited about it.

But then Nick remembered what had happened with *frindle*. It stopped him cold. He was sure that if all the kids stopped buying lunch, sooner or later someone would figure out that it was all Nick Allen's idea. He would get in trouble. People would write about it in the newspaper. The principal would call his parents— anything could happen.

So for the first time in his life, Nick kept a good idea to himself. He never even told John or Chris.

And that changed Nick.

His mom was the first to notice. "Are things okay at school, honey?" she asked one day in early March. He had seemed kind of down, a little sad. It worried her.

"Sure," said Nick. "Everything's fine."

"Everything's okay with your friends? They haven't been hanging around here very much."

"Mom, honest. Everything's fine. It's winter. Everyone's really busy with hockey and basketball—that's all." And Nick went to his room and shut the door.

Mrs. Granger noticed the change, too. The clever little rascal who had looked her in the eye and said, "But I really didn't have a frindle with me—" that boy wasn't in her class anymore. Now a quieter, more careful Nicholas Allen came into class every day. He did all his work perfectly, didn't speak unless she called on him, and didn't laugh and joke with his friends like he used to. School would be over in a few months, and it seemed like there was nothing she could do to help him.

Toward the end of the year, Nick remembered the letter that Mrs. Granger had asked him to sign on the back when the frindle business was just getting started. The chess game was over, so he was expecting to get that letter from Mrs. Granger any day. But all spring it didn't come, so he thought she must have forgotten about it. Nick was afraid to bring it all up again, but he was dying of curiosity.

So on the last day of school, Nick knocked on Mrs. Granger's classroom door. She was straightening up the textbooks on the bookcases below the windows. Without turning around she sang out, "Come in."

Nick said, "Hi, Mrs. Granger."

Mrs. Granger stood up and turned to face him. "Oh, it's you, Nicholas. I'm so glad you stopped by. I've been meaning to talk to you, and this will save me having to send you a letter this summer."

Nick gulped and said, "That's what I came for—the letter."

Mrs. Granger looked puzzled for half a second, and then she said, "Oh! That letter." Then she paused. "You will recall, Nicholas, that I said I would send you that letter when all this was over . . . and it's not over."

"It's not?" Nick tilted his head to one side, and asked, "When will it be over?"

Mrs. Granger smiled and said, "Oh, believe me, Nicholas. You'll know when it's over. I wanted to talk to you about something else."

She walked across the room and stood about two feet from him. Nick had grown during the year, and their eyes were almost on the same level. Nick noticed that the eyes were softer, but just as powerful. "I've noticed that you've been very quiet for the past few months. You know, Nicholas, you didn't do anything wrong this year. I know a lot of things happened, and a lot of things were said, and you must have had some difficult days here and there. But your idea was a good idea, and I have been very proud of the way you behaved—most of the time."

Nick was embarrassed, but Mrs. Granger kept on talking. "And Nicholas, you have great things to do in this life. I'm absolutely sure you do, and you mustn't let a few hard days trick you into clamming up."

Then Mrs. Granger reached out and shook Nick's hand, and looked him in the face. Her eyes were turned up brighter than Nick had ever seen them before. She said, "Nicholas Allen, I have enjoyed having you as a student. Now you go out there and have a wonderful summer. And I expect to hear remarkable things about you, young man. "

Mrs. Granger watched Nick start to leave. But before he got to the door, he turned and said, "Thanks, Mrs. Granger. You have a great summer, too." Then he grinned and said, "And don't forget to buy some new frindles for next year."

Thanks to his little talk with Mrs. Granger—along with a healthy dose of summer vacation—Nick made a full recovery. He was proud that he had made up a new word, and he enjoyed thinking about all the commotion it had stirred up. That one little word had made fifth grade a year to remember.

Before he started sixth grade Nick was Nick again, and all through junior high and high school and college, he proved it.

For example, two years later, all the school cafeterias in town were serving delicious food at least four days a week, all because of Nick the Consumer. And the state superintendent of schools had made a special trip to Westfield to learn why this little town had the most successful school lunch program in the state.

And in high school, well, the stories about Nick's other adventures could go on and on and on. But that would delay the end of this story, the one that started when Nick was in fifth grade.

Because the end of this story came later—ten years later.

And what was happening to Nick's word during those ten years? Nothing fancy, nothing exciting. Words don't work that way. Words either get used, or they don't. And *frindle* was being used more and more. It was becoming a real word.

fifteen

And the winner
Is . . .

TEN YEARS LATER, Nick Allen was a junior in college. And during November of his junior year, two important things happened.

First, Nick turned twenty-one years old, and the frindle trust fund set up by his father became legally Nick's.

Nick was rich. Nick was very rich. Nick was so rich he couldn't even begin to imagine how rich he really was.

Nick wanted to give his parents some of the money, which they said they did *not* need and would *not* accept. But Nick reminded them that they had always wanted to travel, and they should just think of this as a big birthday present or something. So they accepted.

And Nick also wanted to give some money to his big brother, James—who said he did *not* need it and would *not* accept it. But Nick reminded James that his two-year-old daughter would grow up and go to college someday—and besides, hadn't James once given Nick his whole baseball card collection? So James accepted the gift.

After that Nick went out and bought himself a fast new computer. And about ten new games. And a mountain bike. Then he tried to forget about the money, which is a hard thing to do. But he managed pretty well and kept working on his college degree as hard as ever.

The second important thing that fall was the arrival of a package at the door of Nick's apartment one day—a large, heavy package. It was from Mrs. Granger.

There were three things in the package: 1) a brand-new eighth-edition *Webster's College Dictionary*; 2) a short handwritten note taped to the cover of the dictionary; and 3) a fat white envelope. Turning the white envelope over, Nick saw the name—his name. He had written it there one September afternoon in Mrs. Granger's room after school. Ten years ago.

Nick set the envelope down and gently peeled the note off the front of the dictionary.

My dear Nicholas:

Please turn to page 541 of this book.

Nick grabbed the dictionary and leafed to page 541, his heart pounding. And there between *Friml* and *fringe* he read:

frin•dle *(frin' dl)* **n.** *a device used to write or make marks with ink [arbitrary coinage; originated by Nicholas Allen, American, 1987– (see* **pen***)]*

Nick went back to the note from Mrs. Granger.

This is a brand-new dictionary, the one I recommend that my students use for their homework. And now when I teach them how new words are added to the dictionary, I tell each and every one of them to look up the word frindle.

And, of course, I have sent along that letter I promised to give you when our little battle was over.

And now it's over.

Your teacher,

Mrs. Lorelei Granger

Nick's head was spinning. With shaking hands, he opened the fat white envelope. He pulled out the ten-year-old letter and began to read.

Dear Nicholas:

If you are reading this letter, it means that the word frindle *has been added to the dictionary. Congratulations.*

A person can watch the sunrise, but he cannot slow it down or stop it or make it go backward. And that is what I was trying to do with your word.

At first I was angry. I admit that. I was not happy to see the word pen *pushed aside as if it did not matter. But I guess that if the Latin word for feather had been* frindilus *instead of* pinna, *then you probably would have invented the word* pen *instead. Like the sunrise, some things just have to happen—and all you can really do is watch.*

The word frindle *has existed for less than three weeks. I now see that this is the kind of chance that a teacher hopes for and dreams about—a chance to see bright young students take an idea they have learned in a boring old classroom and put it to a real test in their own world. I confess that I am very excited to see how it all turns out. I am mostly here to watch it happen.*

But somehow I think I have a small part to play in this drama, and I have chosen to be the villain. Every good story needs a bad guy, don't you think?

So someday, I will be asking you to forgive me, and I hope you will.

Nick, I know you like to think. Please think about this: When I started teaching, no one had landed on the moon, there were no space shuttles, no CNN, no weather satellites. There were no video cassette recorders, no CDs, no computers.

The world has changed in a million

ways. That is why I have always tried to teach children something that would be useful no matter what.

So many things have gone out of date. But after all these years, words are still important. Words are still needed by everyone. Words are used to think with, to write with, to dream with, to hope and pray with. And that is why I love the dictionary. It endures. It works. And as you now know, it also changes and grows.

Again, congratulations. And I've enclosed a little present for you.

Yours truly,

Mrs. Granger

Nick remembered Mrs. Granger's eyes, and now he understood what some of those special looks had meant. The old fox! She had been rooting for *frindle* the whole time. By fighting against it, she had actually helped it along.

There was a flat, oblong case in the white

envelope, the kind of case you get when you buy a watch. Nick pulled it out and opened the lid. Inside was something else Nick had not seen for ten years. It was Mrs. Granger's favorite pen, her old maroon fountain pen with the blue cap. And under the clip was a little folded piece of paper. It was another note. A very short note. Just one word: Frindle.

About a month later, something happened over in the old part of Westfield, over where the trees are huge and the houses are small. On Christmas morning, Mrs. Granger's doorbell rang. Mrs. Granger opened the door, but no one was there.

Someone had left a package inside her storm door—a box wrapped in green paper with a red bow and a white envelope taped to one end. She smiled as she stooped down to pick it up.

As she picked up the package she noticed a red, white, and blue Express Mail envelope sticking halfway out of her mailbox next to the doorway. It must have been delivered late on Christmas Eve. She opened the storm door plucked the envelope from the mailbox, and

FRINDLE

then shut both doors and went inside with a shiver.

Mrs. Granger went across the living room and sat on the couch. The express envelope was from the Westfield School District office. It looked important, so Mrs. Granger opened it right away.

It was a letter from the superintendent of schools, a letter of congratulations. A permanent trust fund for college scholarships had been established with a donation of one million dollars "from one of your former students."

It would be called The Lorelei Granger Students' Fund.

Mrs. Granger was sure it was a mistake. Or maybe a prank. A million dollars? Nonsense! She had the urge to pick up the telephone and give the superintendent a call and straighten this out right away.

But this was Christmas morning, and even though the superintendent *was* one of her former pupils, Mrs. Granger decided to wait a day. Couldn't hurt.

Besides, the other package was sitting next to her on the couch, waiting impatiently with its red bow. She opened the envelope first.

It was a little Christmas card with a sloppy note—obviously the work of a fifth-grade boy.

Dear Mrs. Granger:

Your one of my favorite teachers.
Here is somthing I want you to
have.

Sincerly,

A student of yours

Mrs. Granger glared at the spelling mistakes, but then chuckled and shook her head. Kids are always the same, year after year. Here she was in her forty-fifth year of teaching, all set to retire in June. She could hardly remember a Christmas day when she didn't have a present from one of her students.

Mrs. Granger pulled off the red ribbon and tore off the paper and lifted the lid of the box. She expected to find something made of yarn and popsicle sticks, or maybe curly macaroni and glue.

But instead she found an oblong case covered with blue velvet. She opened the case and inside was a beautiful gold fountain pen. She picked it up, and it was cool and heavy in her hand. Words were engraved along the pen's shiny barrel, and Mrs. Granger had to slide down to the end of the couch and turn on her reading lamp. Then she could read the three thin lines of type:

This object belongs to Mrs. Lorelei Granger, and she may call it any name she chooses.
                    —With love from Nicholas Allen

SNEAK PREVIEW

Coming from Simon & Schuster Books
for Young Readers in Spring 1999:

THE LANDRY NEWS

A brand-new school story from
the author of

FRINDLE

CHAPTER 1

NEW KID GETS OLD TEACHER

"CARA LOUISE, I am *talking* to you!"

Cara Landry didn't answer her mom. She was busy.

She sat at the gray folding table in the kitchenette, a heap of torn paper scraps in front of her. Using a roll of clear tape, Cara was putting the pieces back together. Little by little, they fell into place on a fresh sheet of paper about eighteen inches wide. The top part was already taking shape—a row of neat block letters, carefully drawn to look like newspaper type.

"Cara, honey, you *promised* you wouldn't start that again. Didn't you learn one little thing from the last time?"

Cara's mom was talking about what had happened at the school Cara had attended for most of fourth grade, just after her dad had left. There had been some problems.

"Don't worry, Mom," Cara said absentmindedly, absorbed in her task.

Cara Landry had only lived in Carlyle for six months. From the day she moved to town, during April of fourth grade, everyone had completely ignored her. She had been easy for the other kids to ignore. Just another brainy, quiet girl, the kind who always turns in assignments on time, always aces tests. She dressed in a brown plaid skirt and a clean white blouse every day, dependable as the tile pattern on the classroom floor. Average height, skinny arms and legs, white socks, black shoes. Her light brown hair was always pulled back into a thin ponytail, and her pale blue eyes hardly ever connected with anyone else's. As far as the other kids were concerned, Cara was there, but just barely.

All that changed in one afternoon soon after Cara started fifth grade.

It was like any other Friday for Cara at Denton Elementary School. Math first thing in the morning, then science and gym, lunch and health, and finally, reading, language arts, and social studies in Mr. Larson's room.

Mr. Larson was the kind of teacher parents write letters to the principal about, letters like:

Dear Dr. Barnes:

We know our child is only in second grade this year, but please be *sure* that he [or she] is NOT put into Mr. Larson's class for fifth grade.

Our lawyer tells us that we have the right to make our educational choices known to the principal and that you are not allowed to tell anyone we have written you this letter.

So in closing, we again urge you to take steps to see that our son [or daughter] is *not* put into Mr. Larson's classroom.

Sincerely yours,

Mr. and Mrs. Everybody-who-lives-in-Carlyle

Still, *someone* had to be in Mr. Larson's class; and if your mom was always too tired to join the PTA or a volunteer group, and if you mostly hung out at the library by yourself or sat around your apartment reading and doing homework, it was possible to live in Carlyle for half a year and not know that Mr. Larson was a lousy teacher. And if your mom didn't know enough to write a letter to the principal, you were pretty much guaranteed to get Mr. Larson.

Mr. Larson said he believed in the open classroom. At

parents' night every September, Mr. Larson explained that children learn best when they learn things on their own.

This was not a new idea. This idea about learning was being used successfully by practically every teacher in America.

But Mr. Larson used it in his own special way. Almost every day, he would get the class started on a story or a worksheet or a word list or some reading and then go to his desk, pour some coffee from his big red thermos, open up his newspaper, and sit.

Over the years, Mr. Larson had taught himself how to ignore the chaos that erupted in his classroom every day. Unless there was the sound of breaking glass, screams, or splintering furniture, Mr. Larson didn't even look up. If other teachers or the principal complained about the noise, he would ask a student to shut the door, and then go back to reading his newspaper.

Even though Mr. Larson had not done much day-to-day teaching for a number of years, quite a bit of learning happened in room 145 anyway. The room itself had a lot to do with that. Room 145 was like a giant educational glacier, with layer upon layer of accumulated materials. Mr. Larson read constantly, and every magazine he had subscribed to or purchased during the past twenty years had ended up in his classroom. *Time, Good*

Housekeeping, U.S. News & World Report, Smithsonian, Cricket, Rolling Stone, National Geographic, Boys' Life, Organic Gardening, The New Yorker, Life, Highlights, Fine Woodworking, Reader's Digest, Popular Mechanics, and dozens of others. Heaps of them filled the shelves and cluttered the corners. Newspapers, too, were stacked in front of the windows; recent ones were piled next to Mr. Larson's chair. This stack was almost level with his desktop, and it made a convenient place to rest his coffee cup.

Each square inch of wall space and a good portion of the ceiling were covered with maps, old report covers, newspaper clippings, diagrammed sentences, cartoons, Halloween decorations, a cursive handwriting chart, quotations from the Gettysburg Address and the Declaration of Independence, and the complete Bill of Rights—a dizzying assortment of historical, grammatical, and literary information.

The bulletin boards were like huge paper time warps—shaggy, colorful collages. Whenever Mr. Larson happened to find an article or a poster or an illustration that looked interesting, he would staple it up, and he always invited the kids to do the same. But for the past eight or ten years, Mr. Larson had not bothered to take down the old papers—he just wallpapered over them with the new ones. Every few months—especially when it was hot and humid—the weight of the built-up paper would become too much for the staples, and a slow avalanche of clippings would lean forward and whisper to the floor. When that happened, a student repair committee would grab some staplers from the supply cabinet, and the room would shake as they pounded flat pieces of history back onto the wall.

Freestanding racks of books were scattered all around room 145. There were racks loaded with mysteries, Newbery winners, historical fiction, biographies, and short stories. There were racks of almanacs, nature books, world records books, old encyclopedias, and dictionaries. There was even a rack of well-worn picture books for those days when fifth-graders felt like looking back at the books they grew up on.

The reading corner was jammed with pillows and was sheltered by half of an old cardboard geodesic dome. The dome had won first prize at a school fair about fifteen years ago. Each triangle of the dome had been painted blue or yellow or green and was designed by kids to teach something—like the flags of African nations or the presidents of the United States or the last ten Indianapolis-500 winners—dozens and dozens of different minilessons. The dome was missing half its top and looked a little like an igloo after a week of warm weather. Still, every class period there would be a scramble to see which small group of friends would take possession of the dome.

The principal didn't approve of Mr. Larson's room one bit. It gave him the creeps. Dr. Barnes liked things to be spotless and orderly, like his own office—a place for everything, and everything in its place. Occasionally he threatened to make Mr. Larson change rooms—but there was really no other room he could move to. Besides, room 145 was on the lower level of the school in the back corner. It was the room that was the farthest away from the office, and Dr. Barnes couldn't bear the thought of Mr. Larson being one inch closer to him.

Even though it was chaotic and cluttered, Mr. Larson's class suited Cara Landry just fine. She was able to tune out the noise, and she liked being left alone for the last two hours of every day. She would always get to class early and pull a desk and chair over to the back corner by some low bookcases. Then she would pull the large map tripod up behind her chair. She would spread out her books and papers on the bookshelf to her right, and she would tack her plastic pencil case on the bulletin board to her left. It was a small private space, like her own little office, where Cara could just sit and read, think, and write.

Then, on the first Friday afternoon in October, Cara

took what she'd been working on and without saying anything to anybody, she used four thumbtacks and stuck it onto the overloaded bulletin board at the back of Mr. Larson's room. It was Denton Elementary School's first edition of *The Landry News*.